Dear Parents and Educators,

Welcome to Penguin Young Readers! As parents and educators, you know that each child develops at his or her own pace—in terms of speech, critical thinking, and, of course, reading. Penguin Young Readers recognizes this fact. As a result, each Penguin Young Readers book is assigned a traditional easy-to-read level (1–4) as well as a Guided Reading Level (A–P). Both of these systems will help you choose the right book for your child. Please refer to the back of each book for specific leveling information. Penguin Young Readers features esteemed authors and illustrators, stories about favorite characters, fascinating nonfiction, and more!

Dick and Jane: We Work

LEVEL 2

GUIDED
READING
LEVEL **E**

This book is perfect for a **Progressing Reader** who:
- can figure out unknown words by using picture and context clues;
- can recognize beginning, middle, and ending sounds;
- can make and confirm predictions about what will happen in the text; and
- can distinguish between fiction and nonfiction.

Here are some **activities** you can do during and after reading this book:
- Compare/Contrast: In the story "Funny Sally," both Sally and Father are working. How is their work the same? How is it different? In the story "Who Can Help?," both Jane and Father help out. How is the way in which they help the same? How is it different?
- Make Predictions: Use the pictures as clues to make predictions. On page 8, what do you think Dick will do next? What will happen to Spot? On page 12, what do you think Sally will have to do next? On page 16, what do you think Father will say to Sally? On page 28, what else do you think Sally, Dick, and Jane will make?

Remember, sharing the love of reading with a child is the best gift you can give!

—Bonnie Bader, EdM
  Penguin Young Readers program

*Penguin Young Readers are leveled by independent reviewers applying the standards developed by Irene Fountas and Gay Su Pinnell in *Matching Books to Readers: Using Leveled Books in Guided Reading*, Heinemann, 1999.

Penguin Young Readers
Published by the Penguin Group
Penguin Group (USA) Inc., 375 Hudson Street, New York, New York 10014, USA
Penguin Group (Canada), 90 Eglinton Avenue East, Suite 700, Toronto, Ontario M4P 2Y3, Canada
(a division of Pearson Penguin Canada Inc.)
Penguin Books Ltd, 80 Strand, London WC2R 0RL, England
Penguin Ireland, 25 St Stephen's Green, Dublin 2, Ireland (a division of Penguin Books Ltd)
Penguin Group (Australia), 707 Collins Street, Melbourne, Victoria 3008, Australia
(a division of Pearson Australia Group Pty Ltd)
Penguin Books India Pvt Ltd, 11 Community Centre, Panchsheel Park, New Delhi—110 017, India
Penguin Group (NZ), 67 Apollo Drive, Rosedale, Auckland 0632, New Zealand
(a division of Pearson New Zealand Ltd)
Penguin Books, Rosebank Office Park, 181 Jan Smuts Avenue, Parktown North 2193, South Africa
Penguin China, B7 Jaiming Center, 27 East Third Ring Road North,
Chaoyang District, Beijing 100020, China

Penguin Books Ltd, Registered Offices: 80 Strand, London WC2R 0RL, England

Library of Congress Control Number: 2003016830

ISBN 978-0-448-43409-4   10 9 8 7 6 5 4 3 2

Dick and Jane
We Work

Penguin Young Readers
An Imprint of Penguin Group (USA) Inc.

Contents

Chapter 1
Work

Work, Dick.

Work, work.

See, see.

See Dick work.

Oh, Dick.

See, see.

Oh, oh, oh.

Chapter 2
See Sally Work

Work, work, work.

Sally can work.

See Sally work.

Oh, Dick.

Oh, Jane.

See, see.

Sally can work.

Oh, Sally.

Funny, funny Sally.

Oh, oh, oh.

Chapter 3
Funny Sally

See Father work.

Work, work, work.

Father can work.

See Sally work.

Work, work, work.

Sally can work.

Oh, Father.

See, see.

Sally can work.

Oh, Sally.

Funny, funny Sally.

Chapter 4
Who Can Help?

See Jane.

Jane can work.

Jane can help.

Jane can help Mother.

Jane can help Mother work.

Father can help Jane.

Chapter 5
See It Work

Father said, "Look, Sally.

See something big.

You can see it work.

Up, up it comes.

See it work."

Sally said, "See it work.

Work, work, work."

"Help, help," said Sally.

"See my little Tim go down.

Jump down, Father.

I want my little Tim."

"Oh, Sally," said Father.

"I cannot jump down.

I cannot help you."

"Oh, see it work," said Dick.

"See it come up, up, up.

Up comes Tim to Baby Sally."

"Up, up," said Sally.

"Up comes my little Tim.

Up comes Tim to Sally."

Chapter 6
We Make Something

"Look here," said Dick.

"I can make something funny.

I can make Spot.

Spot is red and blue."

"Oh, Dick," said Jane.

"I want to make something.

I want to make something blue."

"Look, Sally," said Jane.

"See my funny blue Puff.

Make something, Sally.

Make something blue."

"Oh, Jane," said Sally.

"I cannot make Puff.

I cannot make Spot.

I want to make little Tim."

"See me work," said Sally.

"I can make something blue.

See my funny blue Tim."

"Look, Sally," said Jane.

"Here is something for Tim.

Here is a funny red mother.

And a funny blue father.

A father and mother for Tim."

Chapter 7
Spot Finds Something

Dick said, "Come and work.

Come and help me.

I cannot find the two boats.

I cannot find my red ball.

Where is my yellow boat?

Where is the blue boat?

Where is my little red ball?

Where, oh, where?"

Jane said, "I can work.

I can find two boats.

Here is the yellow boat.

Here is the blue boat."

Sally said, "I can find cars.

See my little yellow car.

See my red car and my blue car.

Where is the red ball?

Where is my little Tim?"

Dick said, "Spot can work.

Spot can find the red ball.

Spot can help me."

Sally said, "See Spot work.

Spot can find Tim.

Spot can help me."